Vampire Limericks and Other Bits of Humor

by Carl Scott Harker

An Aldouspi Publication

Table of Contents

Introduction

With a last name of Harker, it should be to no one's surprise that I have an interest in vampires. Starting with Bram Stoker's "Dracula" when I was 12, I have read many classic novels like Le Fanu "Carmilla." I have devoured countless other vampire stories including "Sherlock Holmes Vs. Dracula" by Loren D. Estleman, Fred Saberhagen's Dracula novels and "I Am Legend" by Richard Matheson. And let's not forget Anne Rice's Lestat and Laurell Hamilton's vampire hunter stories. And no matter how many blood sucking anthologies I have read, I am a sucker for the next one that comes along.

Then there are the movies and tv shows like Bela Lugosi playing Dracula and all the Hammer vampire flicks. There is "Blacula" and George Hamilton's take on The Count. "Buffy, the Vampire Slayer," "Twilight," "True Blood," "The Munsters," "Vampire Diaries" and so many more.

Imagine my shock, when I did a search online for vampire limericks and found almost nothing! I decided to try my hand at filling this soulless void in the world of poetry with a few vampire limericks of my own.

While my nest of undead limericks is fairly small, I think they well represent the more basic mythology of the vampire world that even the most casual reader of vampire literature will recognize. There is also, I hope, an element of humor and story within each 5-line poem. As of 11/01/24, I have added more vampire limericks, since the original publication.

To make this a book, I did need more material, and thus have included, other, more general limericks, some cartoons I have drawn along the way and a short story featuring the works of Edgar Allan Poe. As these works span several different years, I have also included commentary between the different poems and cartoons to keep things in context. Enjoy!

Vampire Limericks

I. Not Necessarily in That Order

The subtle art of seduction

Is the vampire's means of induction,

    To become the undead

    You are taken to bed,

For orgasms, death and some suction.

There are many stories about vampires and how you become one – some say that a vampire might viciously attack you, drain your body of blood and then casually push your body aside and fly away. You are then temporarily dead, but within 24 hours or so, you will awaken as a newly recruited member of the Nosferatu.

Other stories tell of a more romantic creature of the night – one looking for a relationship. Such a vampire lures you into its clutches by seduction. This vampire may give you one last night of great sex or maybe several nights of great sex, while taking small amounts of blood from you. Then after the vampire is sure your are worthy of talking to for the next 1000 years, the creature will seduce you again, suck more of your blood, then ask you to drink its blood in return.

You normally die the next day, sometimes of a broken neck, but usually from anemia. Again, you awaken after 24 hours – as a vampire with a friend. Or more accurately, you and your vampire sire are now "blood lovers" which is a closer relationship than the traditional bonding of "blood brothers or blood sisters." This relationship goes well, at least, until you meet each other's family...

The title in the above limerick "Not Necessarily in that Order" refers to the last line of the limerick. The usual order of events is orgasms, suction and death. I rearranged this order to make the final rhyme.

And now on to the next limerick...

II. Tonight's Meal

Look deep in my eyes and see

Is eternity waiting for thee?

You think I'm your lover,

But soon you'll discover,

You're just a quick snack for me.

About this poem: First let me say that nothing makes you feel more like a poet than when you get to use the word: "thee" in a poem. It makes you feel so Shakespearean.

I remember my early days starting off as a young poet in poetry school. I was a hard poetic worker and studied hard. Then came the day I knew I was ready to use the word, "thee." Still my teacher had to give me official permission.

What a fond memory is that moment, when I stood up in class, with my hand over my heart, feeling a bit of trepidation and lots of youthful pride and sang out my question, "Oh, Sir, can I thee?"

Anyway, back to this limerick, the vampire referred in the poem is one of the brutish kind that just sees people as food. They use a little glamour to entice one into a moment of intimacy and then, wham – snack time!

III. For My Ophthalmologist

Leaving the room up ahead is Count Dracula

Who resembles the actor Scott Bakula

    Now because of the sun,

    He so speedily runs,

He will not register onto your macula.

This limerick uses the tenet that Vampires are harmed or killed by sunlight and thus must hide from the sun's rays at the approach of a new day. Not all vampire legends keep these creatures bound to the night, but it is very common theme. These beings are also known for their ability to travel very fast.

Another basis for this poem is that I have had two cataract removal surgeries, so writing a limerick for my ophthalmologist seemed the natural thing to do. Thus the title and the reference to the macula. For you who don't know, the macula is an area of tissue in the center of the retina by which we can see images straight in front of us.

Finding two rhymes for Dracula was a challenge. "Macula" was fairly easy to come up with and fit my visionary quest. But the name Scott Bakula made the limerick possible.

The actor Scott Bakula came to national fame with his hit TV show, "Quantum Leap," a series about time traveling that also starred Dean Stockwell. The show is intelligent and heartwarming and well worth viewing. Bakula currently (2020) stars in a TV show called "NCIS New Orleans."

IV. I'm Jewish

So you thought you would get my blood,

With a nick of my vein it would flood

    Down your throat it would rush,

    But now what is this mush?

From a Golem you only get mud!

This vampire limerick is told from the viewpoint of a Golem who is being attacked by a vampire.

A Golem is an artificial man created from clay and/or mud. From Jewish folklore, a man-sized statue is sculpted from clay and is brought to life by inscribing the Hebrew word for "truth" on the statue's forehead. In some tales, a scroll with the magic word is placed into the statue's mouth which also works to animate the Golem.

Created to be an instrument of justice, the Golem usually ends up doing more harm than good and becomes a monster.

In this poem, the Golem is inwardly laughing at the vampire who is trying to draw blood from him. Indeed, the Golem is actually mocking the poor being who now has a mouth full of mud, because the Vampire did not recognize that the Jewish monster was not one of his typical victims. (The foolish vampire was then torn apart.)

V. It's All In The Neck

We are known as the beings of the night,

And no mirrors can capture our sight,

Our elongated fangs,

Pierce a vein, that brings,

Eternal life, if the bite, is just right!

This limerick needs little explanation. The title echoes a similar phrase,"It's all in the wrist." Basically, some vampires have that special knack for increasing their brood, others just make a bloody mess.

VI. Where Shall We Eat Tonight?

Vampires feed on the multitude

At the malls, shops and bars for their fortitude,

The occasional blind date,

Those rock concerts are great,

And Blood Banks are first rate for fast food!

2024 is a great time to be a vampire, not only are there more cattle, I mean people, than ever before, these tasty treats are milling about everywhere. And now, most of them won't look up from their phones and tablets long enough to notice a vampire is opening their jugulars.

In the bad old days, a vampire might have to work several nights just to get to first bite, not to mention all that hassle of turning into a mist to slip through cracks in windows and doors. Times change.

VII. Blood and Guts

There once was a vampire named Borman,
Who hid out for a while as a corpsman.
    And sometimes she tried,
    So not every sailor died,
But she was really just there for the gore, man!

This limerick was originally published in my book "Am I Indigenous and other Poems," but in the updated version of this book I decided to throw it in here, too.

The next two vampire limericks were written after I had "finished" the book – first poem was for the cover and the second one went into the sales copy.

Do Vampires Like Poetry?

Difficulties abound when you become undead
The fainting at blood when your fangs first embed,
    And yes! by dawn you must,
    Find your bed or be dust,
But a subject of limericks is our greatest dread.

***

A Lifetime Lease

On obtaining the vampiric seal
Precious blood you will learn how to steal,
    So give it a try
    You just have to die,
To make immortality real!

Another update (2024): I can't help myself I keep writing new vampire limericks… Here are two more!

Period Vampire Limerick

Your presence here brings me delight
As we meet in the last of twilight
    Now you shout that us vamps
    Always bring on your "cramps?"
I will fix that with an arterial bite!

Craving Institutional Recognition (A Vampire Limerick)

Yes, I need the red blood in your vein
But egos, too, must be sustained,
    So why can't this old vamp
    Since dead, appear on a stamp?
"Forever" goes well with my name.

And just to prove I can write poems other than limericks here is a vampire poem in free verse:

Summery of a New York Times Article on the Vampire Dilemma

The vampire population bigger than ever!

A 3.2 percent increase this year,
8.6 percent the year before
Well above

The FVSC – Federal Vampire Suppression Commission's
Mandated target, maximum, low 2% annual increase
In the number of blood suckers amongst us,
Meanwhile the VIRS – Vampire Internal Retribution Service
Can't get the necessary funding
To hire more heart stakers
Because of the Republican blockage in Congress.

The climate crisis has not helped either,
Millions of trees burning up
In national forests
Has raised the cost of a hardwood stake
To 20 times the price of a small silver cross,
Additionally, a strange fungus is attacking
Garlic crops.

There is hope, though, from scientists at the CDC
Who now endorse the President's proposal
That all citizens become vegetarians,
The latest human test data confirms
That vampires are allergic
To anyone
Who has a high level of
Vegetable protein
In their blood.

-30-

Well, this is the end of the vampire limericks + poem, but more limericks follow. Before we get to those, I want to share a vampire cartoon with you on the next page.

Years ago, when I owned a newspaper, an issue popped up concerning a large Christian Cross on top of a prominent hill that was also city property. This controversial cross clearly violated the separation of church and state. Was the city promoting a religion?

The conflict was eventually resolved by the city selling the property to a private party. But before that resolution, I made the following cartoon which suggests a different reason for letting the cross stay on the hill.

Star Trek Humor/Parody

That Remarkable Vulcan Spock Limerick

That remarkable character Spock

Well renowned for his logical talk,

His blood, it is green,

And he never gets mean,

Is most known for his long, pointed "ears."

Yes, I know that the last line of this limerick does not rhyme - it is, thus, illogical to call this a limerick, ha ha! - it is a Vulcan joke/poem.

And if you don't like that explanation for this poem's ending, how about this rationalization: In the original Vulcan language version, the last word does rhyme.

Ok, ok, if you are still not satisfied and need that last line to rhyme, substitute the following line for the fifth line above:

"And exclaims 'fascinating,' not 'grok.'"

The word "grok" comes from Robert Heinlein's great science fiction novel *"Stranger in a Strange Land."* The hero, a human named Valentine Michael Smith, is born on Mars and raised by Martians. He comes to earth, and in the story, become a pop phenomenon whose catch phrase is the word "Grok." During the 1960's, when Star Trek originally aired, using the word "grok" was in!

Grok is a Martian word which means means literally "to drink" and figuratively means "to comprehend," "to love," *and* "to be one with." It is an empathetic and intuitive way to know someone or something, as in "I grok you." Hopefully, you now *"grok"* this poem.

2 Star Trek Cartoons

The *"Deep Space Nine* Star" Trek tv show was unusual as the stories typically took place on a space station rather than a starship as all of the other Star Trek series featured. One of the most interesting DSN characters was Odo, a shape shifter. This cartoon is a variation on the theme of having a "bad hair day."

Before I go further, I want you to know that most of the cartoons in this book were produced via an old Macintosh, circa 1996 or so, using a drawing software program called Art Dabbler. I don't have the program anymore – it either got lost on some crashed machine or it just did not update when the Mac OS updated. I really enjoyed learning to use it, but the digital art files that I still have are not all of the best quality.

Note: This is just my way of saying, "If you don't like the way the art looks, don't blame the artist (me), blame the program."

Some of the cartoons included here are just rough drafts, though - on those you can blame me. With my artistic confession aside, here is the second Star Trek cartoon.

While Vulcans may seem cold and unemotional, their hands can be very expressive!

Random Limericks

– A House on the Hill Limerick with variations! –

A House on a Hill

There once was a house on a hill
Which had several glorious sills,
    Where the pigeons would sit,
    And deposit their shit,
If that house was alive it would kill.

If you happen to be reading this book with a child, you may have hesitated while reading this limerick. That is understandable as it contains a vulgar scatological word, ie "shit. " For those who have sensitive minds or ears, I have created several variations of this poem using the following words to replace "shit:" *Scat; Droppings; Poop; Feces and Blather.* I tossed in "blather" to show that you do not even have to be slightly vulgar!

A House on a Hill (Variation 1)

There once was a house on a hill
Which had several glorious sills,
    Where bats often sat,
    And deposited their scat,
If that house was alive it would kill.

A House on a Hill (Variation 2)

There once was a house on a hill
Which had several glorious sills,
    Where birds came stopping,
    And deposited droppings,
If that house was alive it would kill.

A House on a Hill (Variation 3)

There once was a house on a hill
Which had several glorious sills,
    Where birds would troop,
    And deposit their poop,
If that house was alive it would kill.

A House on a Hill (Variation 4)

There once was a house on a hill
Which had several glorious sills,
    Where numerous species,
    Deposited feces,
If that house was alive it would kill.

A House on a Hill (Variation 5)

There once was a house on a hill
Which had several glorious sills,
    Where birds would gather,
    And blather and blather,
If that house was alive it would kill.

More Miscellaneous Limericks

Having just finished a section of scatological limericks, I hope you don't mind, if I show you another one. The person, who became the US president in 2017, inspired this:

I. President Trump

The President known as Trump
Came riding on an elephant's rump,
But the way that he acts
Using lies as facts,
Makes him more like an elephant's dump.

***

Most people don't associate limericks with social or political issues. Limericks are usually reserved to a higher cause – making people laugh. Still they can be used to reflect current or historical events. The following poem encapsulates a real life event when four students were killed and nine others injured at Kent State University, during a protest demonstration against the Vietnam War in 1970.

II. War Protest

There once were some students from Kent,
Whose minds held an outraged content,
But the National Guard,
Took a stance that was hard,
And their bullets conveyed what they meant.

***

And finally, I provide an example of a dirty limerick.

III. A Dirty Limerick

There once was a laddy named Hurdy

Who often fell down and got dirty,

    His mommy would laugh

    And give him a bath,

I can't help what your mind thinks is dirty!

***

IV. Murderverse – A Husband's Excuse

There once was a husband named Pullet

Whose therapist told him to "Cool it!"

    But he shot his wife

    During domestic strife,

Then told cops, "They were only love bullets!"

Many years ago, I wrote the above poem in hopes that it would be published in *"Ellery Queen's Mystery Magazine."* Unfortunately, the editor disappointed many readers, by rejecting it. I cannot recall if the hybrid word "Murderverse" was my invention or a gimmick used by the magazine – I hope it was me.

***

V. Obtaining Warp Drive

Black holes maybe huge warps in space

Through we'll travel, time to time, place to place,

    But it won't become real,

    If we happen to kill,

The Earth's only sentient race.

We CAN spread the species into space, first by populating the solar system and then beyond. Or to paraphrase the Cowardly Lion of Oz: "I do believe in space, I do believe in space!"

***

VI. Reversed A Rendition

A remarkable woman named Hanley
Whose courageous deeds were so "manly"
    Reversed a rendition,
    Of the marriage tradition,
And her husband became Mrs. Hanley.

Sometimes to impress a woman I was going out with, I would come up with a limerick using her name. In this case, there was a woman I dated whose last name was Hanley and thus the creation of this poem. Of course, she was actually quite feminine in features and deed, but try finding a rhyme for "Hanley!"

Despite the theme of the limerick, she was impressed with my efforts and I did go to bed with her. Which is why poets are considered romantics or, sometimes, just real lucky.

***

VII. Girls of Science

There once was a girl named Kay

Who really just wanted to play

But some old fuddy duddies

Said stick to your studies

And a Nobel Prize is Kay getting today!

***

VIII. Desert Scenario

We have entered the nuclear age

And with missiles a war we may wage,

It seems moot to repeat

That the humans defeat,

Will be great for the ants and the sage.

***

IX. A Vulgarity at Sea World

To a boy spoke the dolphin named Fifi

From the pool with a very loud EEE-EEE,

To all else besides Lilly,

The sounds would be silly,

As she asked the boy not to go pee-pee!

Sea World is an animal park dedicated to creatures of the sea, where a visitor can see dolphins and seals and other water creatures. The name "Lilly" refers to a scientist, Dr. John C. Lilly, who was well-known for his research into the language of dolphins.

***

X. Keep Your Mind on the Road

There once was a trucker named Harker

Who was a notorious sparker,

    But he did not survive

    One night's romantic drive,

When in haste, he'd forgotten, to park her.

Creating limericks from a person's name is always a challenge. It certainly was for my own last name. While the above limerick is okay, I was forced to rely upon a rather archaic word, "sparker" to make the poem work. Sparker is another way to say "lover."

***

XII. Three Fat Old Men

Three fat old men went on a diet

It certainly was good that they try it,

    But their moans and groans

    As they 'came skins and bones

Was broke by big meals at the Hyatt.

This is the kind of limerick you might get from an advertising agency, touting that a good place to eat is at a restaurant in a Hyatt Hotel.

***

The next poem is something that you might find in the psychological section of a job application:

XI. Q. 10 Which Last Line of the Limerick Describes You Best?

There once was a clerk on the phone

Who kept dialing the same busy tone

    It was not a real call

    It was used as a stall

A) An initiative found on his own.

B) But his work was enough to atone.

C) If the taxpayers knew, he'd be stoned.

D) And his boss's attention was thrown.

***

And finally, here are two actual naughty limericks...

XIII. Red Velvet Sash

The girl in the red velvet sash

Would shock others by giving a flash

    Of her figure divine

    Her breasts, oh sublime

And the best was her red velvet snatch.

The image of a red velvet sash infers that this sexy woman is wearing a robe of some kind which she likes to open to reveal her naked body.

***

XIV. A Masturbator's Reason

When asked if he wanted to swing

He replied that he'd once had a fling,

    But his dick was abused

    By his multiple screws,

He stays home now and does his own thing!

This last limerick is an autobiographical one. Ha! Ha! Ha!

You are now finished with the "literary portion" of this book. It is now time to turn to the artistic section...

What follows is a random collection of some of my cartoons. Some were drawn on a computer and some are just rough sketches. Onward to the next page.

Random Cartoons

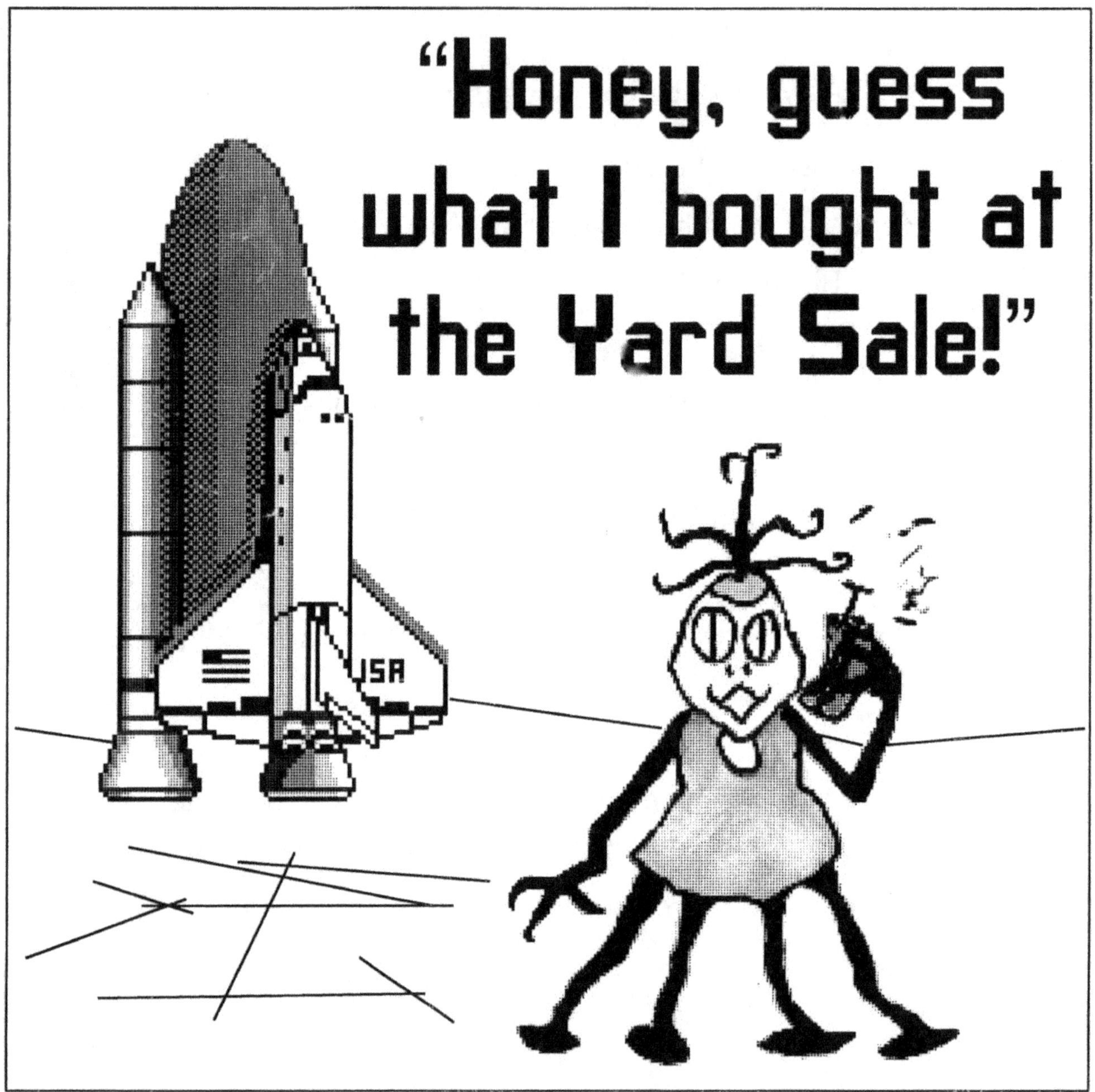

NASA's next generation space shuttle **Dream Chaser** is supposed to be in operation and delivering cargo soon. That will be a great day. But for right now, we can only guess what has happened to any old shuttles left over.

Here is a space exploration cartoon. I believe that one day, humanity will mine the assteroid belt out beyond Mars.

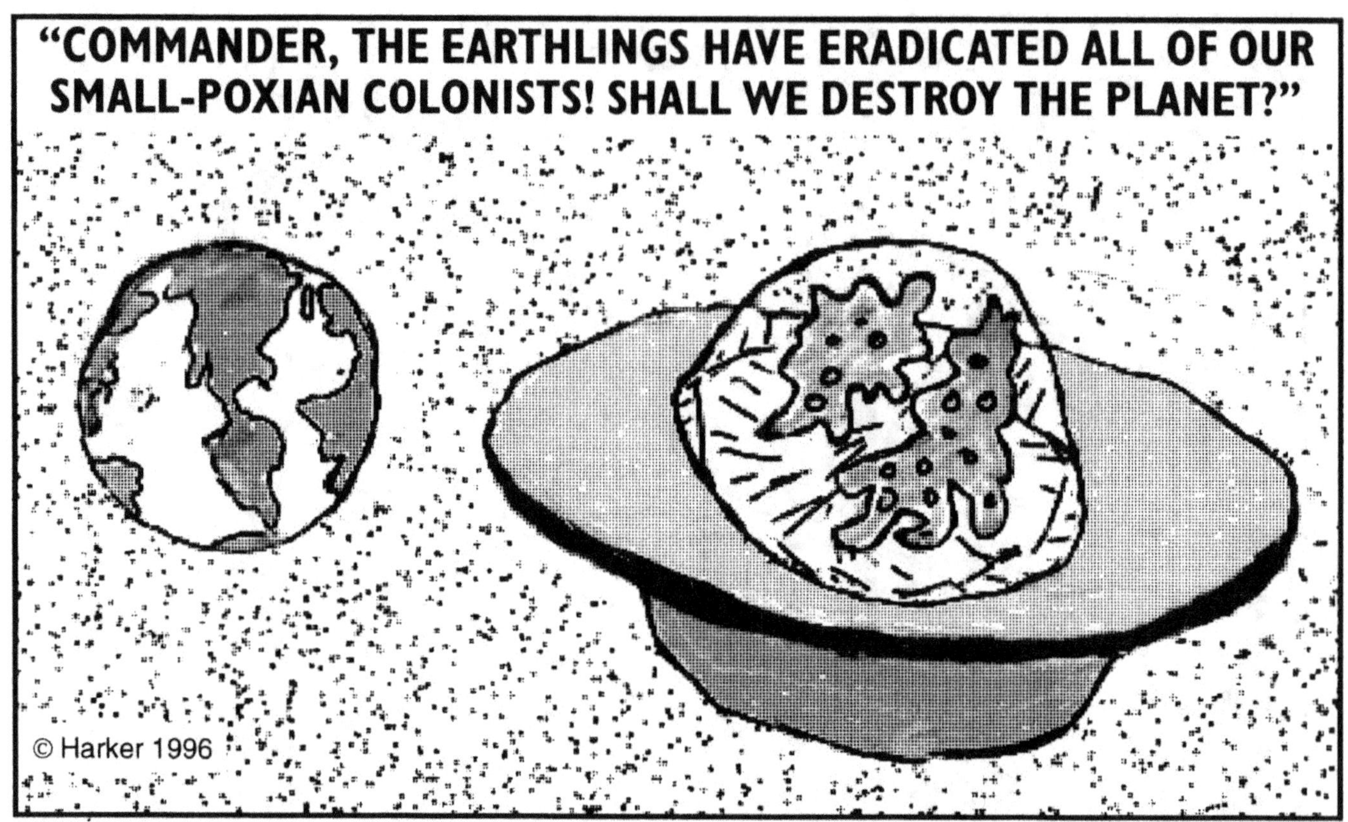

Smallpox was a deadly virus that killed around 33% of those who contracted the disease. Through intelligent vaccination campaigns, the disease was officially eradicated by 1977.

There are some frozen vials of the virus stored in heavily secured labs in the United States and Russia – just in case new vaccines are needed.

Perhaps, such vaccines will be revived, if intelligent viruses from outer space decide to take revenge as suggested above.

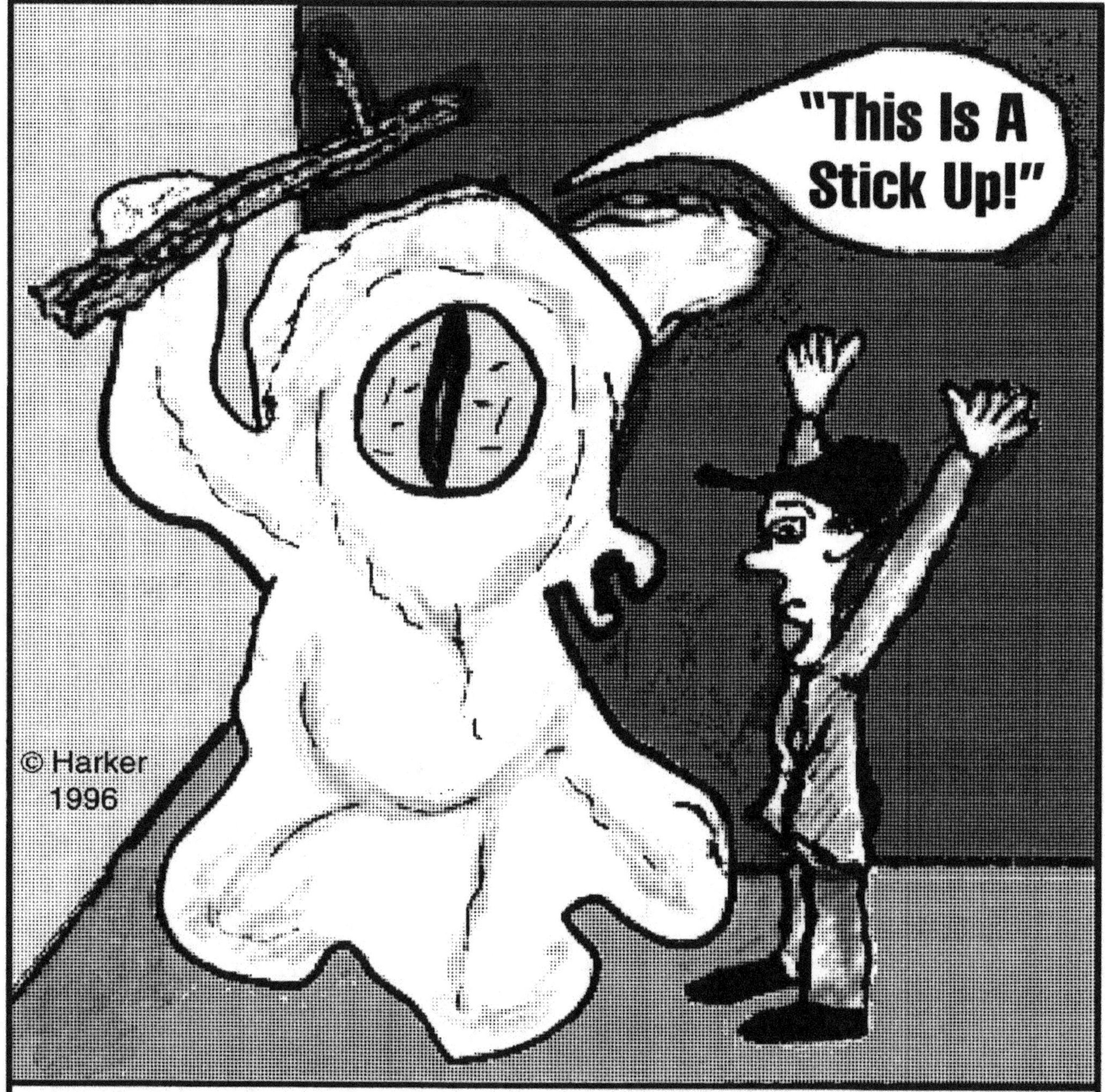

This Extraterrestrial Has Not Quite Grasped Some Of The Subtleties Of Being A Criminal On Earth!

It is fun drawing extraterrestrials, and no one can judge the "quality" of the drawing – because no one knows what visitors from outer space actually look like. Perhaps they really are all blobby and rough looking?

A Rough Sketch

The word ballon says: "My ambition is to change the world."

Around 1992, I was legally blind for 11 months after two botched eye operations. I could see well enough to get around, but I was unable to drive. I managed to get a job at a nearby laundry mat where I monitored washing machines, helped customers, cleaned and closed up a night. In my free moments, I sketched out some laundry mat cartoons like the one above featuring the change machine – and this rough sketch of a cartoon about dryers.

Word balloon L: "How dry I am... How..."

Word balloon M: "They call the wind Maria..."

Word balloon N: "Tumbling, Tumbling, Tumbling, Tumbling, Tumbling, Tumble Weeds"

Word balloon O: "Dan, can't you see that big oak tree..."

Here is a California (earthquake country) variation on the "Falling Rock Cartoon"

Notice how the big brother in the front seat and the little brother in the back seat looks so much alike? Ah, the magic of copying and pasting.

Updated Note (2024): While not intentional when drawn years ago, this car looks much like the latest EV model from Tesla .

I am pretty pleased with how this drawing turned out - especially the bald Lieutenant. The cans in the drawing is just one drawn can copied, rotated and pasted all over. (More computer magic.) I really admire cartoonists who can draw infinite details by hand in their work.

By the way, I am a staunch environmentalist – I coined the word "ecotastrophe" around the year 1971. I think it is a great word for describing the world today – which is one big ecological catastrophe.

"Whose Gang Are You With?"

Wall tagging by street gangs has been an urban problem for quite sometime, but dogs have been tagging their environment for hundreds of thousands of years.

The dog in this cartoon is based upon a favorite pet of mine that was mixture of a terrier and a dachshund. She was a great mouser and was trained to remove people's hats on command.

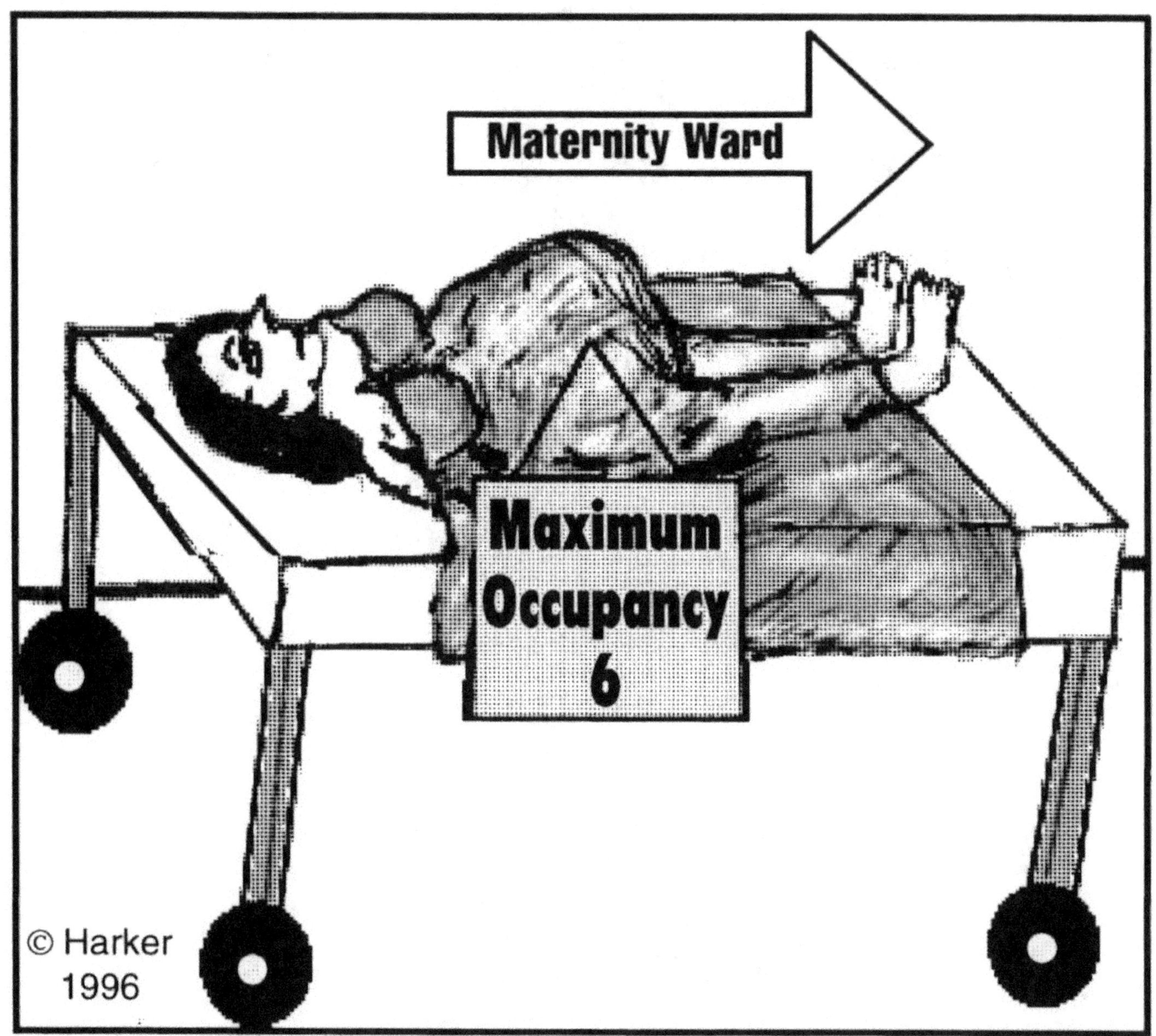

I once worked for the civilian portion of the Oakland Fire Department. That is where I learned that the Fire Marshall has the authority to determine how many people can occupy a particular space.

Caption in the cartoon reads: "Finally! They're thinking about our minds!" This is a rough sketch, but I think it is good enough to get its point across.

KITCHEN SUICIDE #7:
A Long, Cold Death!

© Harker 1996

This is another variation on a standard theme. As a student of comedy, I really enjoyed drawing the bananas.

We are pretty laid back in the state where I live in – this is the kind of Victim's Rights legislation we would probably pass...

FYI, "slupos" are chips covered with melted cheese placed in a pool of soda.

Dungeon scenes, as in this Political Cartoon, is another standard of cartoonists.

Here is a gross question for you: "Does the rat have four legs with two of them hidden in the drawing or has the rat been tortured, too?"

Of course, who would torture a rat? My guess is the same person who would torture people.

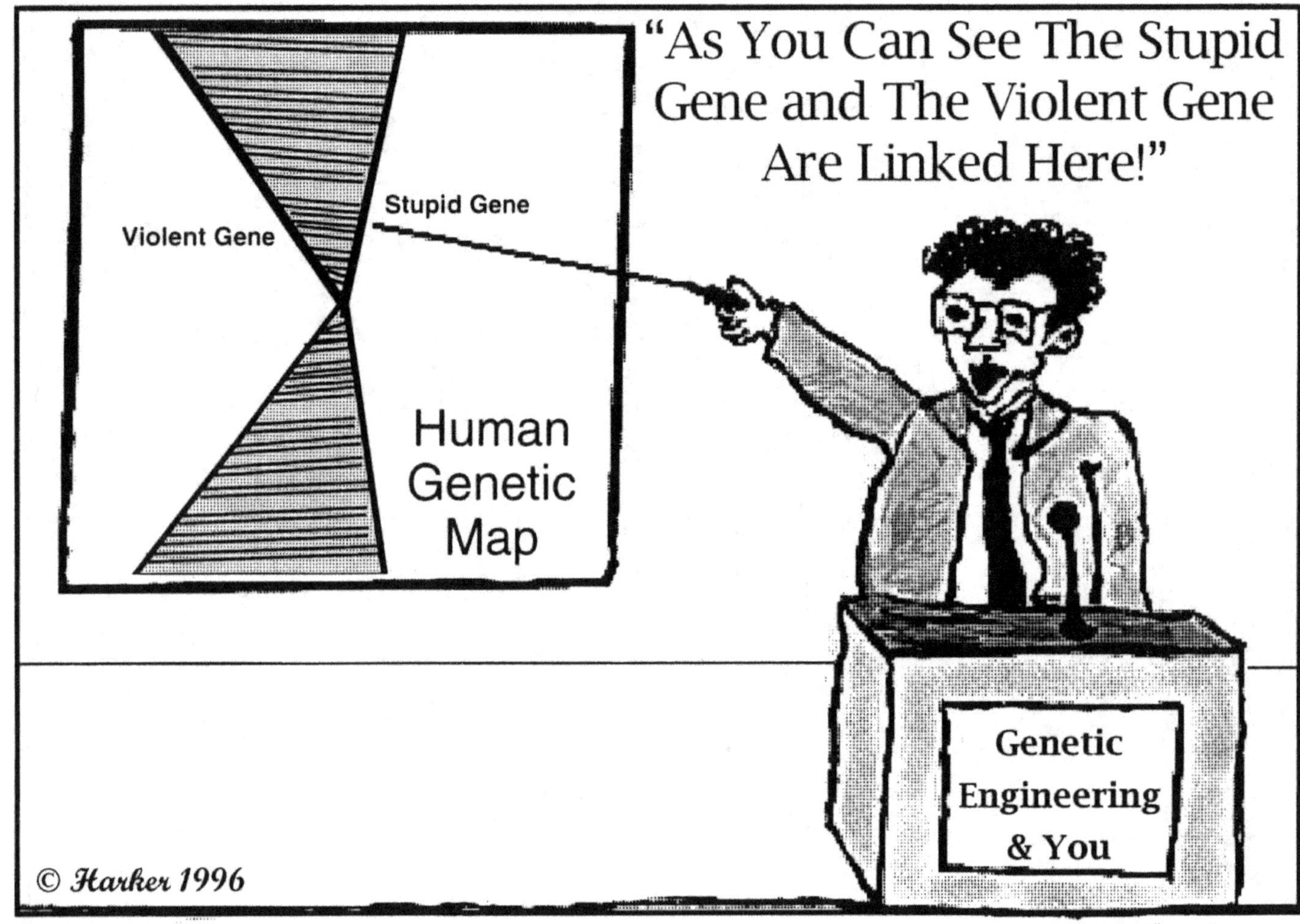

This is one of the lesser known discoveries made while unravelling the human genome.

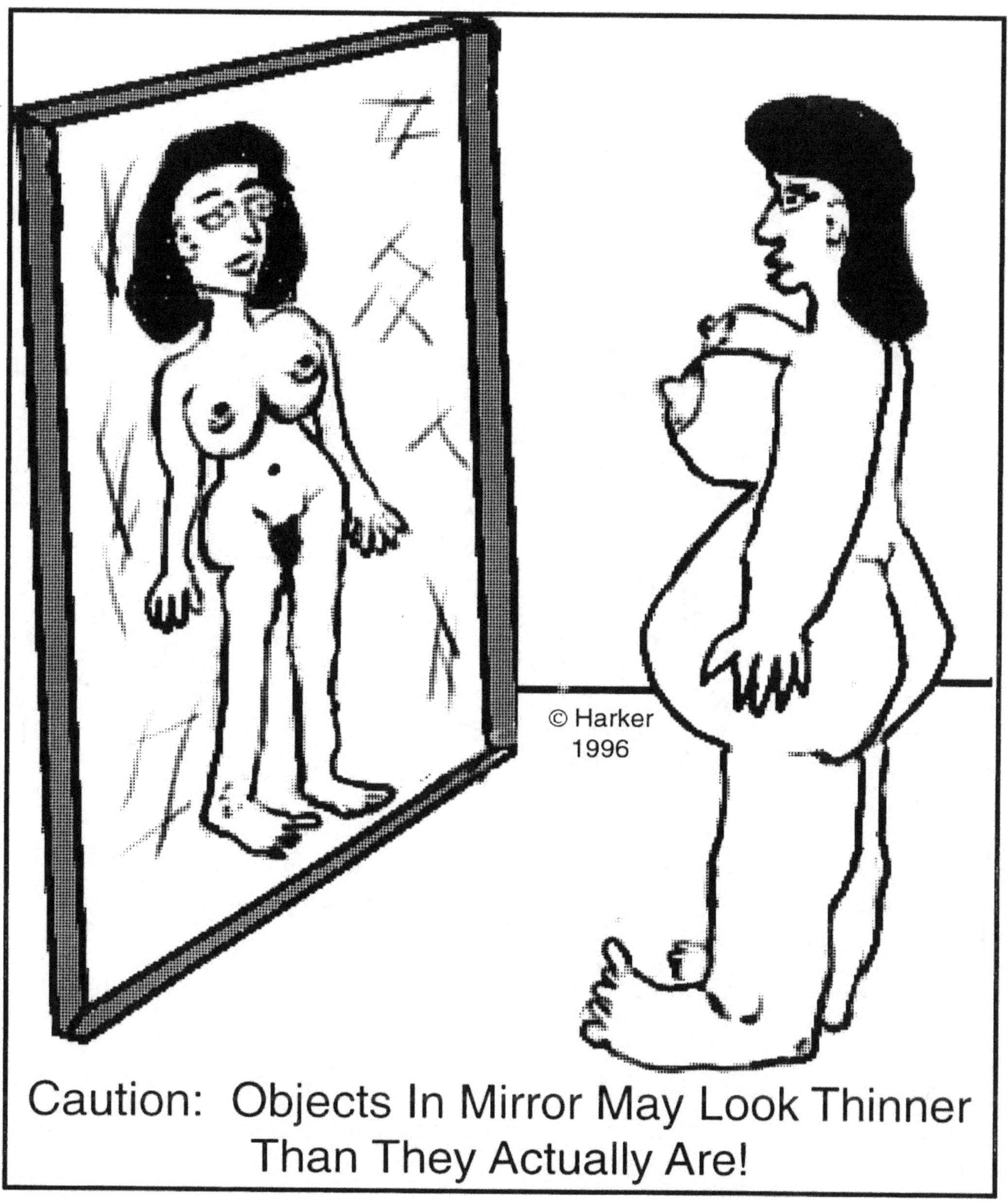

Caution: Objects In Mirror May Look Thinner
Than They Actually Are!

Throughout history, it has been the artist's duty to produce nude images of men and women, whenever they can!

Headstone caption: "Carl S. Harker, 1953 – 2003, Based on a True Story."

As of 2024, I am still here – above ground and kicking. This is just a rough sketch for my epitaph. Headstone humor is another traditional cartoon theme. By the way, 2003 was a difficult year.

If you do not get the joke here, ask one of your Catholic friends.

The Farewell Kiss

– A short story based on the works of Edgar Allan Poe –

Why will you say that I am insane? True, I am nervous, very nervous, and the throbbing and pounding of my heart ever increases. It is just that misfortune has plagued me like the padding of black cats. But I am not yet Raven Mad.

If only the steel and glass clock upon the mantle did not constantly tick and tock of her death, a week ago this hour. For "she is gone" is the thought which ever echoes in the chamber of my brain. And my brick emotions, walled in and chained forever to my despair, have taken me to the brink whose fall ushers in the house of madness.

But still I refuse the eerie music and do not yet dance at the Masqued Ball in the wings of this cracked house. "Oh, she is gone," is the shriek uttered through the maelstrom in the anguish of my aloneness. This must end, but how? Ah, with a Kiss, and say goodbye to the lost Lenore. Goodbye to the lost Lenore. Too long have I tarried from the marbled mausoleum, the tent of internment where likes the sleeping Lenore. Make haste!

I enter now her greasy crypt, panning the scene, gazing at the wilted, spicy flowers, going down the battered and baked steps, touching the caked and crumbling walls of her prison. A chill enters me, icing my bones. And I know, no matter what happens, the ingredients of my eternal recipe will change, and I shall never be the man I was.

A movement! She lives! NO! But a Gold Bug which I crush beneath my heel.

There she lies, pale, motionless, as if dreaming of fairy lands and the crystal palaces of Paladin. To awaken soon and tell my trembling ears of the flickering spectral dances of the spirits of her soul...

But these, too, are dangerous thoughts. For here, the Conqueror worm is king and hurries to fill his cask with the wines of her body. He hastens to wither her breasts, to shrivel and crack the cerulean eyes that once met mine. The blood congeals, the skin thickens, yellows, rots, to leave white bones behind.

But still Lenore's form is firm. And now for the Kiss. Wait! What is this? Already, a foul, moldy reek slips out from her faded lips. A fetid and malodorous breath oozes like a grey and slimy fog from her mouth, coming towards me, a thing unclean. What terror is this that festers and corrupts the body and discolors the mind? My brain melts at the thought of touching this abomination of life. To be defiled, become impure, to be swept into the cesspool of unholy deeds, the vortex of the breaking seeds of insanity.

I, too, am lost, caught between the pit of my original despair and this pendulum of perpetual changing horror. Yet, give not my hope, a premature burial. For from the book of the Necromancer, *Delenda Est Mortius*, comes a secret solution, an elixir of miraculous power to sweeten and stay the taste of death. Here in this crystal vial, is this amber liquid, this mouthwash, Nevermore®, guaranteed to refreshen and disinfect, so one doesn't have to be concerned over close contact.

I pour in the contents of the fragile vial, I always carry with me. It is working, a green froth bubbles up from her mouth, destroying the taint of corrupt flesh. I kiss her, fresh as a day in spring. I am at Peace, thanks to, Nevermore®.

***

History of "The Farewell Kiss:" This homage to Edgar Allan Poe was written one late night in 1975, when I was working as a night attendant at an insane asylum. The piece, in different versions, has been performed as a monolog on college campuses, on the radio, on the stage and it has also appeared elsewhere in print.

Originally, I performed this piece as part of an ensemble of comedy skits performed by the comedy group, *Nobody Imparticular*. Since then, I have performed it in front of theater audiences in California and elsewhere in the country. It is a lot of fun to read out loud – try it!

About the Author

The author currently resides in a small coastal town in Southern Oregon where he owns a small photography publishing business. He is also busy writing poetry and stories as well as pictorial books of art and illustrated poems.

More Books by the Author

 **"A Gustav Klimt Sampler"** – Here is a collection of 46 paintings and drawings by the Austrian artist Gustav Klimt. This is a sampling of his best work. The book is available on Amazon at https://amzn.to/3TPS1FK.

 **"Classic Art of Absinthe"** - This book collects the best of the classic artwork about absinthe from the makers of absinthe, those who wanted absinthe banned and the artists of the time (mid-1800's to early 1900's). It is available on Amazon at https://www.amazon.com/Classic-Absinthe-Carl-Scott-Harker/dp/1653501189.

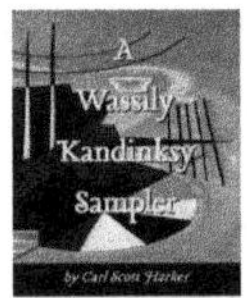 **"A Wassily Kandinsky Sampler"** – This art pictorial collects the best of the abstract artist Wassily Kankinsky, one of the funder of abstract art. It can be found on Amazon here: https://amzn.to/4dqBBgc.

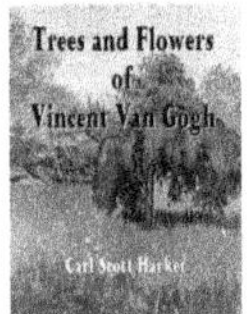 **"Trees and Flowers of Vincent Van Gogh"** – This book collects the best examples of trees and flowers painted by the artist /Vincent Van Gogh. Here is the link for this pictorial book: https://amzn.to/3p3aall.

 **"An Engineer of Words"** – This twelfth book collects a selection of poems written between January 1, 2022 and August 31, 2022. There are story poems, biographical poems, silly poems, poems that rhyme and many that do not. You will find this book here: https://amzn.to/3DFchDI.

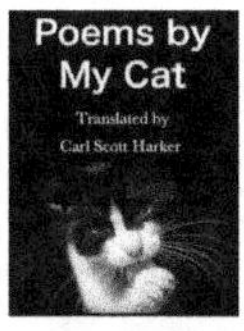 **"Poems By My Cat"** – These poems reveal how cats view the world. The book can be found on Amazon here: https://www.amazon.com/Poems-Cat-Carl-Scott-Harker/dp/1793903239.

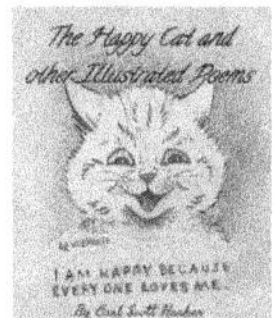 **"The Happy Cat and other Illustreated Poems"** – This book collects aClassic Cat Art accompanied by original poems. Here is the link to the book on Amazon: https://amzn.to/4aqYBKa.

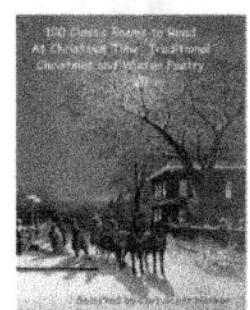 **"100 Classic Poems to Read at Christmas Time"** Here is a collection of some of the best Christmas poems written. The book can be found here: https://www.amazon.com/dp/B07J9YS7QK

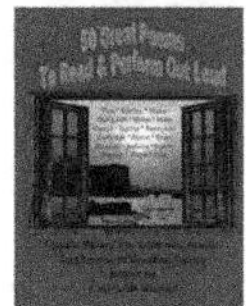 **"50 Great Poems to Read & Perform Out Loud"** - This is a collection of some of the best poems ever written in the English language. The book can be found here: https://amzn.to/2zz8GFT.

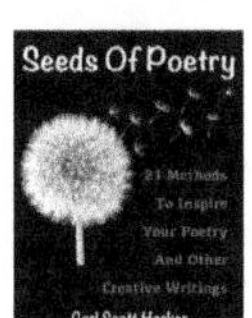 **"Seeds of Poetry: 21 Methods to Inspire Your Poetry and Other Creative Writings"** – a book featuring writing tips with examples to inspire the writing of your own poetry and other creative works. You will find this book here: https://amzn.to/2HtMpO7.

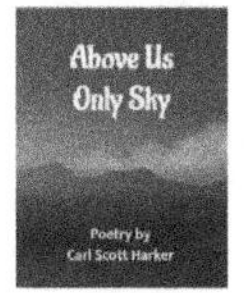 **"Above Us Only Sky"** – This book of poetry features poems written between late April, 2020 to late October, 2020. You will find this book here: https://amzn.to/38kb83R.

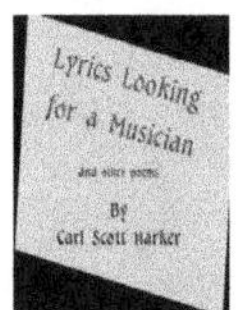 **"Lyrics Looking For A Musician and other poems"** – This collection of poems is a chronicle of the days between June 1st and the end of December, 2021. You will find this book here: https://amzn.to/3x1kjU6.

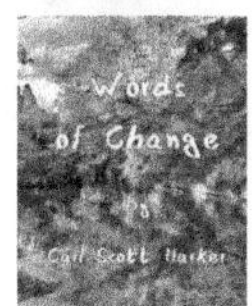 **"Words of Change"** – This book of poetry features poems written from late October of 2020 through May, 2021. You will find this book here: https://amzn.to/3Kxzjy2.

 **"The Hedgehog and Other Selected Poems"** – Here is a collection of illustrated poems for children that adults will enjoy, too. Here is the link: *https://amzn.to/4afXXA8*.

 **"Poems of Personal Poverty"** – Here is a collection of poems that explore material poverty in the midst of spiritual wealth. Here is the link: https://amzn.to/42PvcHc.

 **"The Mad Artist: A Sherlock Holmes Story in Free Verse"** This book presents a new Sherlock Holmes story and is written in free verse and features the artist Vincent Van Gogh. It is available on Amazon at https://amzn.to/36nWvf0.

 **"Frankenstein's Monster in Oz"** - This book tells the story of how Frankenstein's Monster comes to Oz and what happens to him there. It is available on Amazon at https://www.amazon.com/Frankensteins-Monster-Carl-Scott-Harker/dp/1707291365.